Shhhh

by Clare Barron

‖SAMUEL FRENCH‖

FOR PRODUCTION INQUIRIES

UNITED STATES AND CANADA
info@concordtheatricals.com
1-866-979-0447

UNITED KINGDOM AND EUROPE
licensing@concordtheatricals.co.uk
020-7054-7298

Each title is subject to availability from Concord Theatricals Corp., depending upon country of performance. Please be aware that *SHHHH* may not be licensed by Concord Theatricals Corp. in your territory. Professional and amateur producers should contact the nearest Concord Theatricals Corp. office or licensing partner to verify availability.

SHHHH was first produced by the Atlantic Theater in New York City in January 2022. The performance was directed by Clare Barron, with intimacy coordination by UnkleDave's Fight-House, dramaturgy by Agnes Borinsky, sets by Arnulfo Maldonado, costumes by Kaye Voyce, lighting design by Jen Shriever, and sound design by Sinan Refik Zafar. The Production Stage Manager was Laura Smith. The Assistant Stage Manager was Thomas Dieter. The Props Supervisor was Samantha Shoffner. The cast was as follows:

WITCHY WITCH	Constance Shulman
KYLE	Greg Keller
SHAREEN	Clare Barron
PENNY	Janice Amaya
FRANCIS	Nina Grollman
SANDRA	Annie Fang

CHARACTERS

WITCHY WITCH – Fifties or older. A sexy, shy, charismatic postal worker who's been out of the dating game for a while. Also, a witch. She loves her sister Shareen, deeply.

KYLE – Late twenties to late thirties. Thinks of himself as a kind person but is deeply careless. Impulsive. A strange mix of generosity and selfishness.

SHAREEN – Late twenties to early thirties. Slowly malfunctioning. Behavior that was cute in her early twenties is getting decidedly less cute. In a lot of pain. She loves her sister Sally, deeply.

PENNY – Twenties to forties. Shy, incredibly kind weirdo. Into kink. Tentative but funny and warm. Bad things have happened to them, but it hasn't made them bitter.

FRANCIS – Early twenties. Very sexually experienced for her young age and knows what's up.

SANDRA – Early twenties. Recovering from a traumatic sexual experience that has made her feel old. Sensitive and soulful but still funny and biting.

AUTHOR'S NOTE

Notes On Offstage Casting

Either Francis or Sandra can play the role of **ROOMMATE**.

Also, the final stage direction (minus the last paragraph) should be heard by the audience as the final text of the play. In our production, we worked the text into the sound design and had someone record it, but there are a lot of ways you can go about it.

Notes On The Play

This play was written in the spring of 2016 before the #MeToo movement erupted. It was also written before I had fully processed an experience of sexual assault in my own life. The play was my attempt to arrive at a name for what had happened.

Trauma in this play is buried and comes out in strange ways. All the characters except Kyle have experienced some kind of sexual violation that has left them feeling fucked up and bad. They talk about it casually, though. And the play doesn't want to be morose.

The pronouns listed in the script reflect the version of the play we did for the New York world premiere. If there are actors, however, who relate to a character's experience and want to play them, feel free to change the pronouns to suit. If you have questions about this, contact your licensing representative at Concord Theatricals.

We worked with the amazing UnkleDave's Fight-House for intimacy coordination, and I would suggest not doing this play unless you have someone you trust overseeing this aspect of the production.

Finally, Witchy Witch's spells (Scenes 1 and 6) are based on ASMR, and our sound designer Sinan created a whole "ASMR in the theater" set up with a microphone and carefully placed speakers, etc. to magically mimic the effect.

1.

Darkness. We hear in the dark...a whisper.
Up close, intimate, electronic. We can hear the
lips, teeth, saliva, etc.

WITCHY WITCH.

Hi.

...

...

...

...

How are you doing today?

...

...

Thanks for being with me

...

...

Today I just want to provide you with

some simple sounds

...

Made from random objects

...

Around my house

...

And allow you just to listen

...

To the sounds of them

...

And *relaxxxxxx*

...

Do whatever you need...

...

...

...

...

...

...

I started a ritual where I clean off the table

that I'm working on

...

With a Lysol Wipe

<the soft sound of a cloth wiping a table>

I know a lot of you like the sound of wiping sounds so this
is for you

<the wiping sound continues>

I think that anything that has to do with cleaning

...

Has a real calming effect on the brain

...

...

Just letting everything go...

...

Wiping it away...

<the wiping sound continues>

<she breathes in>

Smells like lemon-mint

...

I love iced mint tea in the summers, don't you?

...

...

<the sound of a cup sliding

across a wooden table>

I'm actually drinking some hot tea right now

...

...

Lavender-chamomile

...

Have you ever tried lavender tea?

...

I love it so much

...

...

It's like drinking hot perfume

<light, breathless giggle>

No it's much better than that

...

...

I'm drinking it out of a ceramic –

...

Coffee cup

...

...

Do you hear it?

<the light pings of fingernails tapping

against a ceramic mug>

My grandmother gave me this cup

...

There's little bears on it

...

With little fuzzy tails

...

And little fuzzy bellies

...

...

...

...

...

...

It's hot

I have to blow

<the sounds of her blowing air across the hot water and
then of a little slurp; and then another little slurp>

You know what goes so well with hot tea?

...

...

...

Biscuits

I have a little box of biscuits right here

<the sound of plastic crinkling; she tickles her fingers all
over the biscuit's packaging; this goes on for a long time>

The packaging is in Italian

...

i Cereali

ricchi di fibra

con fiocchi d'avgnon

...

...

...

I'm going to open them

<the sound of plastic crinkling>

I don't really like biscuits but it's a sacrifice
I'm willing to make –

...

...

For you

<the sound of her nibbling on a little piece of biscuit>

Mm

...

...

...

So sweet

...

...

It's so nice to have a little snack at the end of the day?

...

...

Don't you think?

<the sound of nibbling>

Indulge yourself

...

...

...

...

...

...

...

You deserve it

2.

Lights up on a man sitting on a toilet, peeing. His penis is tucked inside the bowl. This is KYLE. The bathroom belongs to SHAREEN, who is offstage in the kitchen. We hear her voice as she talks to KYLE in the bathroom – the door slightly ajar.

KYLE. Wait, so I think what happened was –

My friend was out boating. And they were drinking, you know, whatever. And his cousin was on the prow of the boat sunning himself. Which you shouldn't really do on that type of boat because it's just a little speedboat. I mean, it'll practically tip over. And he got up and he was trying to climb back into the boat, around the windshield, and he *slipped* and his arm went straight through the glass, fist first.

SHAREEN. *(Offstage.)* Oooh

KYLE. And the skin from his wrist down to his elbow was sliced off completely

SHAREEN sneezes.

KYLE. I'm talking like a carrot peeler. There were flaps of skin hanging all the way from his wrist to his elbow. Tickling his armpit. But he's still on the prow of the boat, you know. And freaking out and bleeding everywhere, so he falls into the water...

SHAREEN. *(Offstage.)* Oh my god

KYLE. Because it's just a tiny boat and it's slippery. And he's just floundering in the water. Trying to keep his arm above the surface. His skin hanging down his arm like a banana peel. And then, out of nowhere, a boat like three-times the size and going three-times the speed hits him. / Like right in front of my friend's eyes.

SHAREEN. *(Offstage.)* OH MY GOD

KYLE. No! Wait for it. It gets worse. Then the boat, the
bigger boat, starts to back up –

> *SHAREEN sneezes.*

> *She sneezes again.*

KYLE. Cuz they're like: "We hit something!" And my friend
is like *screaming* at the top of his lungs for them to
stop. But it's too late and they reverse over his cousin –

SHAREEN. *(Offstage.)* Oh my god!

KYLE. And when his cousin bobs back up to the surface,
totally unconscious, there's blood *everywhere* and the
boat has *cut through most of his leg*. Like right through
his calf muscle, right to the bone. My friend is like
touching his cousin's muscle and stuff. Trying to stick
him back together. Putting his skin back on like a
fucking Band-Aid.

> *A small sneezing attack from the kitchen.*

> *A voice calls off from a different bedroom.*

ROOMMATE. *(Offstage.)* (Bless you!!!)

SHAREEN. *(Offstage.)* (Thank you!)

KYLE. So they get him to the hospital and everybody's
freaking out so much about this guy's arm and leg,
nobody's really thinking about anything else. So
apparently this guy needs a urine catheter, everybody's
like: "Okay. That's normal. Put one in." Now the way
a urine catheter works is you take this tube / and you
stick it into the tip of the penis, right?

SHAREEN. *(Offstage.)* I know how a urine / catheter works

KYLE. And then you thread it all the way up the urethra
until you hit the bladder. So they're taking this tube
and threading it up, but instead of urine... Straight

blood comes out. Like I'm not talking urine *and* blood. I'm talking pure, on hundred percent, undiluted blood. Like. A lot of it. Like over a liter. And so this guy just starts pissing pure blood straight out of his catheter. And the nurses are like having *a fit* because apparently he had all these internal injuries they didn't even know about yet because everyone was so distracted by his fucking arm.

SHAREEN. ...

KYLE. ...

SHAREEN. Wow...

KYLE. Yeah...

SHAREEN. ...

KYLE. ...

SHAREEN. ...

KYLE. So, anyway, that's the part – the last part – that reminded me of you. Or your health stuff anyway.

SHAREEN. Wait, the what part?

KYLE. I don't know. Just like.

...

...

Mysterious blood.

> *SHAREEN's wandered into the bathroom by that point.*

SHAREEN. Oh. Yeah.

> *She's carrying a handful of raw mushrooms. Her hands are wet.*

KYLE. What are you holding?

SHAREEN. Mushrooms

KYLE. Are you eating them raw???

> *She pops one in her mouth and chews.*

SHAREEN. I love raw mushrooms

KYLE. That's disgusting

SHAREEN. I'm cooking them, too! Are you sure you don't want to stay for dinner?

KYLE. Who's coming?

SHAREEN. Just my sister. And maybe my roommate will join us, I don't know

KYLE. Nah, I should go

> *SHAREEN accepts this and wanders back into the kitchen.*
>
> *A moment of SHAREEN making noises in the kitchen.*
>
> *KYLE puts his head in his hands, distressed by something.*

SHAREEN. *(Offstage.)* Do you ever just try cutting vegetables with your hands?

KYLE. What do you mean?

SHAREEN. *(Offstage.)* I mean. Not using a knife.

> *KYLE is not really interested in this line of questioning.*

SHAREEN. *(Offstage.)* Like just – Tearing them with your hands. Like I'm just ripping up these mushrooms into pieces. It's so satisfying.

KYLE. Yeah, I don't know

SHAREEN. *(Offstage.)* I'm never using a knife again

KYLE gets up slowly. He flushes the toilet. He puts himself back in his pants. He considers washing his hands...

KYLE. Thanks for letting me use your bathroom

SHAREEN. *(Offstage.)* No problem!

KYLE. I was desperate

SHAREEN. *(Offstage.)* I under / stand

KYLE. And I just figured you're always home...

SHAREEN. *(Offstage.)* HA

KYLE. I hope it's not *weird*

SHAREEN. *(Offstage.)* No, no. I'm happy to see you

Kitchen sounds from the kitchen.

And then silence.

SHAREEN comes back into the bathroom and lies down on the floor next to the toilet, her legs on either side of it.

KYLE. You okay

SHAREEN. Yeah. I just needed to lie down for a sec

KYLE. ...

SHAREEN.

...

...

...

I don't like being in the other room when I'm talking to you.

KYLE puts the toilet seat down and sits back down.

SHAREEN. When I sneeze?

KYLE. Yeah?

SHAREEN. It's like the inside of my mouth is one of those
fast-forward flowers from the movie *Planet Earth*?
Except instead of flowers. I'm blossoming snot

KYLE. I'm sorry

SHAREEN. And then I just swallow

KYLE. Ew.

> *SHAREEN laughs.*
>
> *She looks up at him.*

SHAREEN. You get a job yet?

KYLE. Um, yeah

SHAREEN. Oooh what is it?

KYLE. I'm working for MSNBC?

SHAREEN. Doing what

KYLE. Social Media

SHAREEN. They hired *you* to do that

KYLE. Apparently

SHAREEN. That's weird

KYLE. ...

SHAREEN. *(Laughing.)* Not bad! I just don't think of you
as a big "social media guy"

KYLE. Uh, there's like seventeen of us

SHAREEN. You still writing

KYLE. Little bit

SHAREEN. How's your play

KYLE. I don't want to talk about it

How's *your* play

SHAREEN. Haha I don't want to talk about it either

KYLE.

   ...

   ...

   ...

SHAREEN. You're doing good, though?

KYLE. Yeah! I'm doing good. I'm doing excellent.

SHAREEN. That's good

KYLE. What about you?

SHAREEN. I'm doing much better

KYLE. You look better

SHAREEN. Yeah, that's because I'm doing good

KYLE. I'm sorry about your health stuff

SHAREEN. No, no. I'll figure it out

KYLE. ...

SHAREEN. ...

KYLE. ...

   Well, I'm glad to hear you're doing good

      They smile at each other.

SHAREEN. Hey Kyle

KYLE. Yeah?

SHAREEN. I think your toe is touching my vagina

KYLE. Haha yeah

      *KYLE's foot has disappeared inside
      SHAREEN's skirt – her legs still on either side
      of the toilet.*

KYLE. You're not wearing any underwear

SHAREEN. I never wear underwear

KYLE. I know

> *KYLE puts his toe inside SHAREEN's vagina.*

SHAREEN. Oh!

> *She laughs.*

SHAREEN. I've never had a toe inside of me before

KYLE. I've never fucked somebody with my toe

> *He fucks her a little bit with his toe.*

> ...
>   ...
>   ...

KYLE. We were always good at doing new things together.

SHAREEN. I guess we were.

> *He fucks her a little bit with his toe.*

> *And then stops.*

SHAREEN. Are you sure you don't want to stay for dinner?

> *Infinite temptation, and then...*

> *A knock at the door.*

WITCHY WITCH. Hello?

SHAREEN. *(Whispering.)* That's my sister...

KYLE. *(Whispering.)* I'm gonna go

3.

SHAREEN and her sister post-dinner. They've finished eating, and now they're drinking coffee – the kind of coffee you drink after getting drunk. SHAREEN is very high on coffee. She feels like she could chomp on buildings with her teeth. She's bleeding slightly from her nose, and she dabs at it with a handkerchief. Her sister SALLY is a very sad, stately older woman. And also a witch! (She's dressed like one, too.)

SHAREEN. And my hormones are all fucked up. I'm picking out black witchy hairs from my chin with my fingernails, and I'm way too young for that shit, even though, actually, I'm not that young anymore. I mean, look at you! You're only two years older than me and I could've sworn you've aged centuries. Remember when we were both little girls sharing the same bedroom! What the heck happened?

WITCHY WITCH. We got old.

SHAREEN. I hate it.

WITCHY WITCH. But wiser?

SHAREEN. No, you're right. I love it, too.

WITCHY WITCH pours her more coffee.

SHAREEN. And work is a disaster. The television people keep calling me and offering me things and I just want to sit in my room and cry. Have you talked to Mom?

WITCHY WITCH. No. Why?

SHAREEN. Sometimes I think about her in that house, all alone, at like, seven at night, and I just want to die

WITCHY WITCH. Do you mind if I smoke a cigarette in your kitchen?

SHAREEN. Oh

WITCHY WITCH. I'm too lazy to go downstairs

SHAREEN. No. Do it. I like the secondhand smoke

> *WITCHY WITCH takes out her cigarettes.*
>
> *SHAREEN heaves a monumental sigh.*

SHAREEN. I just wish.........

> *WITCHY WITCH lights a cigarette.*

SHAREEN. I could be somebody's pet, you know?

> *WITCHY WITCH smokes.*

WITCHY WITCH. Like in sex?

SHAREEN. No, like in *life*. I just want somebody to tell me when and where I can go to the bathroom.........

   ...
   ...
   ...

You know what I'm saying?

WITCHY WITCH. I'm going to make another pot of coffee

SHAREEN. Thank you

WITCHY WITCH. And put schnapps in it

SHAREEN. I don't have any schnapps

WITCHY WITCH. *(Winking.)* I have it in my purse

> *WITCHY WITCH goes to make another pot of coffee with generous amounts of schnapps.*
>
> *SHAREEN steals WITCHY WITCH's cigarette and smokes.*

SHAREEN. And I've still got the stomach shits...

WITCHY WITCH. I was going to ask about your health stuff...

SHAREEN. I went to the doctor, and he's making me shit into all these little cups and put them in my refrigerator. (Don't look in my refrigerator.)

WITCHY WITCH is peering into her refrigerator.

WITCHY WITCH. Noted

She takes out the cream.

SHAREEN. But it's funny because he says I can't let the shit touch the water so I have to put Saran Wrap across the seat of the toilet and then shit on the Saran Wrap and then collect the sample from that but I don't think the doc understands that *I'm shitting water* so essentially my shit juice is just running all over the bathroom and I'm having to scoop it up, catch it like little waterfalls cascading over the toilet seat before it hits the floor and the other week Kyle and I were fucking –

WITCHY WITCH. Wait, I thought you two were not –

SHAREEN. *No, no, no!* That's totally over.

WITCHY WITCH. Good. I think he's terrible.

SHAREEN. We're just friends.

WITCHY WITCH raises her eyebrows.

SHAREEN. But the other week we were fucking –

WITCHY WITCH. Uh-huh

SHAREEN. And he's just really, I mean in general, he's just really determined to teach me new things about my body?

WITCHY WITCH. *Uh-huh*

SHAREEN. And he thinks all this time I've been cumming the wrong way or that I don't fully understand the vast nature of my cums and so the other week he was trying to get me to squirt just by fingering me *way up* there like up by my cervix he's got very long fingers and I tried to explain to him that I have a backwards vagina and I'm really sensitive to penetration and that I think I'm just the type of gal who cums from her clit and a nice soft tongue but he's determined to show me this new way to cum! So he's digging into me trying to show me I can do it, trying to show me I can squirt for him and at the same time I'm sucking his dick because it makes him hard when a girl sucks his dick at the same moment she's about to cum and he's just digging at me, scraping at me, and I'm getting all cut up and he's just pushing on my cervix and his dick is down my throat and I get so confused about which hole is which hole which hole is my mouth and which hole is my cunt and which hole is my asshole I feel all filled up I just feel this incredible pressure rising and rising and rising and he's saying: *Cum for me baby cum for me!* And I feel this incredible explosion and shit goes everywhere. *Everywhere!* It's on his face, it's on his belly. And still he's just fingering me saying: *Cum for me baby, cum for me!*

WITCHY WITCH. ...

SHAREEN. And then eventually we both just give up and he realizes that I'm not going to cum and we both just lay there, and I'm thinking: I wonder if we just fucked?

   ...

   ...

   ...

Because I have *no* idea what just happened or what was in what hole or what is part of his body or part of mine and then I realize that we are both covered in *liquid shit* and I say: Did you just shit all over me?

WITCHY WITCH. ...

SHAREEN. And he says: I'm so sorry

And neither of us acknowledge that it's mine.

   WITCHY WITCH smokes.

WITCHY WITCH. I think...

> *The kettle whistles.*
>
> *WITCHY WITCH gets up and turns it off.*

WITCHY WITCH. I think...

...

...

You should probably go back to the doctor

> *They sit. SHAREEN dabs her bloody nose.*
> *Somewhere in the distance a church bell rings*
> *nine o'clock. Dong, dong, dong, dong, dong,*
> *dong, dong, dong, dong.*

SHAREEN. You wanna come with me to the Compline Service tomorrow?

WITCHY WITCH. What's Compline?

SHAREEN. Bells. Singing.

WITCHY WITCH. Wait, what's tomorrow again?

SHAREEN. Tuesday

WITCHY WITCH. *(Whispering to herself; wracking her brain.)* Tuesdayyyyyyyyy

SHAREEN. I think there's going to be barley tea and candlelight...

WITCHY WITCH. *(Remembering.)* No, sorry! I've got a date.

SHAREEN. Oh!

WITCHY WITCH. But I'm leading a meditation ritual on *Wednesday*. If you want to come

SHAREEN. Wait, Sally!

WITCHY WITCH. What?

SHAREEN. Who's your date?!

4.

*WITCHY WITCH out on a date with the lovely
PENNY. She's taken PENNY to the Morbid
Anatomy Museum. They both love witchy stuff.*

WITCHY WITCH. I thought it would be bigger

PENNY. No. It's small. It's intimate. I like it

WITCHY WITCH. I didn't realize it was just one exhibit.
I thought they had a whole – I don't know. I thought
they had a whole regular exhibit *plus* other exhibits,
you know?

PENNY. I feel like this is the perfect size. We won't get
overwhelmed

    They stare at something in a case.

PENNY. Is that syphilis?

WITCHY WITCH. Um

    *She refers to her museum "pamphlet" – just a
    stapled-together collection of pages.*

WITCHY WITCH. Number twenty-eight...

    ...
    ...

Yeah. That's syphilis (*She reads the pamphlet.*) On
the tongue

PENNY. Oof

WITCHY WITCH. And there they have it on the genitals

    She points.

WITCHY WITCH. And there they have it on a baby

    She points again.

PENNY. Do you think they used like real babies? And real bodies? To make these? Or is this all just...molded from wax? Like by an artist?

WITCHY WITCH. Well the death masks are –

PENNY. Yeah the death masks are –

WITCHY WITCH. The death masks are definitely from real people

From real *bodies*

But the rest is...

> *WITCHY WITCH flips through her pamphlet, looking for an answer.*

WITCHY WITCH. I don't know

PENNY. I'm gonna pretend that it's all real

> *They peer into cabinets and slowly circle 'round what must be a relatively small room.*

PENNY. *(Whispering from across the room.)* Sally...

> *WITCHY WITCH looks over at PENNY. PENNY points at something. WITCHY WITCH looks. She laughs.*

WITCHY WITCH. Wow.

> *They keep circling. PENNY comes up behind WITCHY WITCH. It's a little sweet and a little sexy. They peer into the case.*

PENNY. *(Almost a whisper.)* My favorite are the birthing... Are the birth ones with the...

...
...
(they stare, mesmerized)
...

PENNY. With the heads coming out of the vaginas. And the forceps

> *WITCHY WITCH smiles*

PENNY. And the one in the center

WITCHY WITCH. The anatomical Venus?

PENNY. Is that what she's called

WITCHY WITCH. I think so

PENNY. She's lovely

> *WITCHY WITCH refers to her pamphlet, suddenly unsure.*

PENNY. There's some really beautiful feathers in the other room

WITCHY WITCH. I feel bad that it's so small

PENNY. No it's the perfect size

I get to look at everything twice

…

…

And there's a gift shop downstairs

WITCHY WITCH. I know. I was looking at it while I was waiting for you

PENNY. Sorry about that

WITCHY WITCH. It was fine

PENNY. Well maybe we can look at the gift shop again after. I love gift shops. Pretty much more than any other kind of shop there is

WITCHY WITCH. Sure

PENNY. Or get a coffee. I'll do whatever you want

4.2

WITCHY WITCH and PENNY out for coffee
after the Morbid Anatomy Museum.

PENNY. And do you like it?

WITCHY WITCH. It's all right

PENNY. Don't you get cold in the winter?

WITCHY WITCH. Sometimes

PENNY. It probably takes longer because you have to walk through the snow

WITCHY WITCH. Yes it takes longer

PENNY. And what about overtime

WITCHY WITCH. *(Shaking her head.)* I only work eight hours

PENNY. But what if you get more mail?

WITCHY WITCH. I don't know. It just always sort of works out

PENNY. Or not enough mail? Do you only work seven hours?

WITCHY WITCH. No. I always work eight hours. I just sort of slow down or speed up my walking

> *WITCHY WITCH smiles. Timing the walking*
> *right takes some skill!*

PENNY. And do you like it?

> *WITCHY WITCH smiles.*

WITCHY WITCH. Sure

PENNY. Do you know the other people?

WITCHY WITCH. The other postal workers?

PENNY. Yeah

WITCHY WITCH. A little bit. I see them in the morning. When we're sorting our mail. And again at night. It's kind of nice. We sort of see each other at either ends of the day

PENNY. That's nice

WITCHY WITCH. But it's pretty lonely

PENNY. Yeah

WITCHY WITCH. It's a pretty lonely job

> ...
> ...

> I requested to get transferred to the forensics department

PENNY. What's that

WITCHY WITCH. Where they test for drugs in the mail. Illegal substances

PENNY. Ooh fascinating

WITCHY WITCH. Yeah, I'd feel like a detective. But I'd have to move to Salt Lake City.

PENNY. Salt Lake City!

WITCHY WITCH. Yeah...

PENNY. That's cool.

> *PENNY daintily sips their coffee.*

WITCHY WITCH. And what do you do?

> *PENNY smiles.*

PENNY. I'm a dog walker

WITCHY WITCH. Oh no!

PENNY. What???

WITCHY WITCH. We're mortal enemies!!

PENNY. Oh no, I would never let a dog bite you. I would never let a dog bite *anyone*.

WITCHY WITCH. That's good.

PENNY.

Do you
remember...........   *(they could say anything;*
....   *WITCHY WITCH waits in*
                                   exultation)

Do you know all the names?

WITCHY WITCH. Of the mail?

PENNY. Yeah. Of the people

WITCHY WITCH. Oh

      She thinks.

WITCHY WITCH. I think if you asked me to tell you right now, I would go blank. But when I see the names, I know them. I know when something's right and I know when something's wrong

...
...
...

Brian Rice

      PENNY laughs.

WITCHY WITCH. That's a name

PENNY. I love you, Brian Rice! I love that name

WITCHY WITCH. ...

PENNY. ...

WITCHY WITCH. What did you think of the museum?

PENNY. I liked it. I'm glad I went

WITCHY WITCH. Maybe we should go to another one

PENNY. Another museum?

WITCHY WITCH. Maybe. Why not

PENNY. *(Hedging.)* Sure

> I'm a little busy right now

> But sure. Maybe in September

WITCHY WITCH. I don't have a lot of people in my life who
I can go to museums with

> *PENNY smiles.*

PENNY. I guess me either

4.3

> *PENNY and WITCHY WITCH are still on
> their date. It's late. The moon is out. PENNY
> is drunk on wine.*

PENNY. I've been going to these sex parties?

WITCHY WITCH. Really?

PENNY. Is this okay to talk about??

WITCHY WITCH. Yes! It's fine!

PENNY. I don't mean to be *weird*

WITCHY WITCH. No, no I'm interested!

PENNY. I'm just like

> Going to these sex parties and –

> It's a pretty big deal to me

> Because like –

> I don't know

> I feel like I'm back in control?

WITCHY WITCH. Uh-huh

PENNY. Like some shitty stuff happened

And now I can go to a sex party

And I don't have to go home with anyone

And so it feels like I'm back in control?

WITCHY WITCH. Where? What kind of parties? Where do you go?

> *They shrug.*

PENNY. I don't know. My friend took me to one of them and then I just like. Met people. And now I go

WITCHY WITCH. But where are they? How does it work?

PENNY. Oh, they're all over the place

They're in the basement of this grocery store

WITCHY WITCH. A grocery store?

PENNY. Yeah the Associated Foods

Well not actually the basement of the grocery store

Just under the grocery store

It happens to be under the grocery store

But it's not the grocery store's basement

WITCHY WITCH. Huh

PENNY. And it's like this dungeon under there

Like this labyrinth

Made out of plywood

With cushions

WITCHY WITCH. And what do you do?

PENNY. Um

WITCHY WITCH. Like who is there

PENNY. People. Everyone is there

And you just...

I don't know

It's nice

You don't have to go home with anybody

It's just sort of about *you* and what you need

It's so nice

> *PENNY smiles to themselves and sips their wine. They're sleepy. They want to go home.*
>
> *WITCHY WITCH clears her throat.*

WITCHY WITCH. If you're ever interested...

I have this...contraption?

PENNY. (*Wine drunk and deliciously sleepy.*) Uh-huh

WITCHY WITCH. I just have to hold onto it, put it anywhere on my body, in my hand, or sit on it so it's touching my thigh and then it makes my fingertips electric?

PENNY. Really?

WITCHY WITCH. So if I touch you and I'm sitting on it or holding onto it, I can give you a little shock? The electricity moves through my fingers. And everywhere I touch you, it shocks you. And I can turn up the dial so it either tickles or hurts. Whatever you want. And then I could touch your arm... your neck... your tongue. I could stick my fingers in your mouth. I could kiss you! I could trail my fingers up-and-down your neck. I could tickle your ass. Or tickle around your pussy. I could take your top off and play with your nipples. And everywhere I touched you it would shock you – either tickle or hurt. Whatever you want.

...

...

Anyway. So you should let me know, if you would ever want to do something like that.

Still so wine drunk and sleepy...

PENNY. Sure, sure

I'm a little busy right now

PENNY smiles at her, their eyes closed.

PENNY. But maybe in September

4.4

WITCHY WITCH alone with a glass of wine under the moon. PENNY has gone home to sleep.

WITCHY WITCH. It's true. I am a postal worker. When I was little and growing up, lots of people's dads and moms were postal workers. But since I moved to the city, I am the only postal worker I know. (Minus the people I work with, of course.) We're a dying breed.

I like it, though.

You get to get close to people's houses. Sometimes you even get *keys* to their houses! Or keys to the vestibules in front of their houses. You get to touch people's mail.

I like it when you get to put your hand upon the doorknob. I like it when you get to go inside the vestibule – and for a moment nobody can see you from the street. I'm scared of dogs. Everything they say about postal workers is true.

I used to touch love letters. I used to touch letters from grandmothers. And slim brown-paper packages. And postcards from far away. I used to be the bearer of sacred objects. The bearer of *news*! Good and bad and boring. I used to have to decipher bad penmanship to figure out which letter went to whom.

Now I am mostly the bearer of junk and of letters that nobody wants and of paper that people will just throw away.

I have a letter from the nineties. I've been holding onto it. It's addressed to one Louis Gonzalo. I found it at the bottom of my bag at the end of a particularly harrowing week. I was so ashamed.

I had forgotten to deliver it. It looked official. It looked like something he should definitely know about. It looked like the invitation to a wedding. I kept it. I don't know why. My shame was so great, I couldn't bear to deliver it a day late. I took it home. I kept it. I still have it. Tucked in my bookshelf, shamefully. I have nightmares about it. It's a federal offense! I imagine the government raiding my apartment and finding this stolen letter and hauling me to jail.

I imagine Louis never getting this tax document or wedding invitation and his friendship crumbling: WHY DIDN'T YOU EVEN RSVP????!!!!!

If I get the job in forensics, I'll have to burn it just to be safe.

> *KYLE hurries across the stage, from Point A to Point B. He's going somewhere! He's late!*

> *WITCHY WITCH watches him suspiciously.*

Excuse me, for a moment. There's someone I have to follow

> *She scurries after him.*

> *The sun comes up. It's lunchtime.*

5.

SHAREEN in a pizza parlor. She's bored. She's waiting for someone. She dumps the various condiments out on the table in little piles – parmesan cheese, basil, chili flakes – licks her finger and then picks up the little flakes of cheese, etc. and places them on her tongue.

Sitting at a table near her are two women who are having a private conversation over pizza and Big Gulps* and who don't give a fuck. They are the only other people in the restaurant.

(Words in <angle brackets> are uttered at a slightly lower volume – still audible, just slightly under the breath.)

SHAREEN eavesdrops.

FRANCIS. So he fucked you without your consent

SANDRA. No

FRANCIS. He fucked you

SANDRA. Yes but he didn't use a condom

FRANCIS. Did you want to use a condom?

SANDRA. Yes. No! I mean, I said it was okay. I totally consented. I said it was okay. But I was *drunk*

FRANCIS. Right

SANDRA. And it was four in the morning. And we were *in the middle* of having sex. And we had had several sober conversations about how important it was for me to use condoms because my sister's cervical cancer was caused

---

* A license to produce *Shhhh* does not include a license to publicly display any branded logos or trademarked images. Licensees must acquire rights for any logos and/or images or create their own.

by HPV and I was feeling very paranoid and also I had this other bad experience with a guy who drunk-fucked me without a condom *also* at five in the morning –

FRANCIS. Did you consent?

SANDRA. Yes! I consented

FRANCIS. Okay, good

SANDRA. But why was he asking, you know????

FRANCIS shrugs and slurps her drink.

FRANCIS. They ask

SANDRA. Anyway the point is I had expressed to this guy why it was really really important to me to use a condom. And we had had a heart-to-heart about it and stuff and he said it was really important to him that I felt *safe* with him, you know, that he wanted to make me feel *safe* and then *he still asks me* at four in the morning if he can just <fuck me> a little without a condom, just a little bit, but not <cum inside of me> and I said, "I don't know," and he asked again, and I said I was worried about it and he reassured me and then we did it and he <fucked me without a condom> *for like a long time* and then at the last second he pulled out and it made me feel scared because I kept thinking...when are you going to pull out? And afterwards I felt nervous but okay and also it was <hot> like he <came so hard> I got <semen> in my eye and he was <fucking me> from behind, you know. But then in the morning I felt awful.

And so, so stupid

......
......

And also this was before he had told me that he had had like one hundred sexual partners and hadn't had an STD test in over three years

......
......

SANDRA. And also he was secretly fucking my friend

FRANCIS. Wow

SANDRA. So, yeah

FRANCIS.

   ...

   ...

   ...

   Was he drunk

SANDRA. Yes. Really drunk

   ...

   Does that make it better? Or worse?

FRANCIS. I don't know

SANDRA. ....

FRANCIS. ....

SANDRA.

   ....

   ....

   Anyway...

   ....

   ....

FRANCIS. Yeah

SANDRA. So I just don't know

   ....

   I just don't know how I should feel

FRANCIS. Yeah

SANDRA. Like how complicit am I?

   Like how much is it my fault?

FRANCIS. I don't think you should think of it in / terms
   of *fault*

SANDRA. Like I consented

But also

I feel hurt

I feel a little violated, you know

I feel violated

I just do. I don't know how to explain it but. I feel violated

FRANCIS. Yeah

SANDRA. I feel like I set my limit and then he asked me to change my limit in a moment where I was drunk and vulnerable and that makes me feel violated. And also angry. Also, I'm angry

FRANCIS. That's tough, man

I'm sorry

They sip their drinks. Slurp!

FRANCIS. Sometimes I think

If someone were to give me a button and say:

If you push this button you could kill

All the Heterosexual Men

In the world

I would be ethically obligated to push that button

SANDRA. Yeah

They think about their ethical obligation to kill all of the heterosexual men in the world.

SANDRA & FRANCIS.

...

...

...

SANDRA. *Yes*

FRANCIS. But then

Here I am

A very privileged white woman

So maybe someone would be obligated to push the button for me as well

> *Toward the end of the above, SANDRA gets up and wanders across the restaurant toward SHAREEN's table.*

SANDRA. *(To Francis.)* Keep talking. I'm gonna get some chili flakes

FRANCIS. No, I'm done

SANDRA. *(To Shareen.)* Hi. Can we borrow this?

> *SHAREEN hands SANDRA the chili flakes, abashedly.*

SHAREEN. No problem

> *SANDRA takes the chili flakes from SHAREEN, returns to her table, and sprinkles them all over their pizza.*

FRANCIS. Not too much

> *They eat and think.*
>
> *A long moment of the women eating pizza, SHAREEN with her cheese flakes, etc.*
>
> *Finally...*

FRANCIS. I don't know

SANDRA. What

FRANCIS. I guess I've just lost any faith that guys like that would ever – I don't know. Be human

SANDRA. Sure

FRANCIS. Like let's see –

Like the first time I had sex it was without a condom.
Like I was dumb. I was seventeen. But the dude. The
dude was twenty-six. And it's like. Who are you. *Who
are you, dude?* What are you doing? And *every* guy.
Pretty much *every single guy*. Not every single guy.
But quite nearly every single guy. Just tries to slip it in.
I'm always like: What're you doing? And they're like:
Oh. Do you want me to use a condom? It's like: *YEAH.*
Duh. We are both promiscuous people. We are drunk.
We are having sex for the first time. It is in your best
interest for you to use a condom. But you know. It's
easier to pass things from male to female. Or maybe
they just don't care, I don't know. Or maybe they're
already infected. With something. I mean, we're all
already probably infected with something so maybe we
should just chill out. I feel like after everybody stopped
freaking out about *dying from AIDS* and DARE and
shit, everybody started just chilling out and taking the
condoms off. But it's not about chilling out. It's actually
about *communicating.* (I'm gonna eat this crust.)

SANDRA. Do it

FRANCIS eats SANDRA's discarded crust.

FRANCIS. It's actually about letting people make their own
decisions. And respecting their bodies

SANDRA. Uh-huh

FRANCIS. And when have men-in-general *ever* respected
female bodies. Yeah no. 2018. We're not even close.
Don't lie to yourself. You are your body. *You are your
body.* You are your ass. You are your tits. I read these
text messages on my friend's phone once – between
him and his guy friend. He thought they were funny
and so he showed them to me. Just all: "Did you see
that girl in class today? Great ass. No tits. Boring face."

It was a ranking system. Just constantly. Just all the
time. Tits. Ass. Face. Tits. Ass. Face. It was a game to
them. I was like: Is this how you think about me? Do
you think about my body like this? They're like: Yes!
But don't worry. You have a very nice ass, legs, etc. I'm
like: *Ew.* They're like: You do that, too! You talk about
men that way, too! I'm like: No. No I don't. I think a
guy is cute. I say he's cute. Like *the whole person. He's
cute.* I don't fucking dissect his body into fucking pieces
like a fucking dead animal.

FRANCIS.
...
...

> *They pick at the pizza carcass.*

SANDRA. I guess it's kind of discouraging when you think
about it

> *SHAREEN has gotten up and wandered over
> to the napkin area to wipe her fingers. (And
> also so she can listen better.)*

FRANCIS. So yeah...

> *FRANCIS looks around the restaurant to
> make sure nobody she's talking about is here.*

<Daniel> tried to fuck me without a condom. <Paul>
tried to fuck me without a condom. <David> tried to
fuck me without a condom. And that's just the last
six months. That's just who I can remember. And by
"try" I don't mean ask. I mean, just went for it. AND
ALSO. This one dude. It's six in the morning. We get
to his place. He's sexy. I'm feeling it. We're kissing. It's
incredible. I want him to fuck my brains out. And he
starts to slip it in, you know. Knock at my door. I'm
like: I think there's something at my door. He's like:
Yeah there's something at your door. I'm like: Do you
have a condom? And he's like: I don't do condoms. And

I'm like: What? And he's like: I don't do condoms. And
I'm like: Ever? And he's like: Yeah, I don't do condoms,
ever. And I'm like: But you have a lot of sex? And he's
like: I'm vigilant about getting tested. Like what the
fuck is that. Vigilant. Like how often, motherfucker.
How often. Like every time you put another skank-ass
pussy like this one in your mouth??? Vigilant about
getting tested. Yeah right. He's just getting the HIV
prick at the free clinic and walking home twice a year.
Fuck you, motherfucker, you don't "do condoms." Fuck
that guy. Seriously *fuck that guy*. Seriously fuck that
guy. And you know it's just because he can't keep it
hard. The problem is not the condom! The problem is
him! The problem is his sick head! It's like. *Oh! I put
the condom on. My dick gets soft*. I've got an idea! Stop
watching porn and learn HOW TO USE YOUR DICK.
Stop *masturbating in your room* all day long and
learn how to keep an erection like a GROWN-UP you
pathetic weak-brained, limp-dicked loser. Jesus Christ.
Just fuck that guy

...
...
...

And you know what I had sex with him

SANDRA. You didn't

FRANCIS. I did

Because I hate myself. And I was drunk

And I'm overly-invested in men thinking I'm sexy.
And sexual

But fuck that guy

Fuck that guy

...

That's one guy I'd like to kill

SANDRA. Yeah

FRANCIS. But fuck me too, you know

>   *They sit.*

SANDRA. I just keep thinking about this moment

FRANCIS. …

SANDRA. I was with these sheep

>   I was in England
>
>   This was after high school
>
>   I took a gap year and got a shitty internet job
>
>   And I went to England
>
>   And I went straight to the moors

FRANCIS. Oh! I always wanted to / go to the moors

SANDRA. You should go

FRANCIS. Oh my god I have to go

SANDRA. And if you go

>   Go in August
>
>   I didn't even realize it
>
>   But I went in August
>
>   And that's heather season
>
>   When the heather is in bloom

FRANCIS. Oh wow

SANDRA. And whole hillsides were lit up with purple

>   The most beautiful color of purple
>
>   Like mauve
>
>   Or there was some gray in it
>
>   Which I find beautiful

FRANCIS. Uh-huh

SANDRA. And not really hillsides

More like cliffs

Cliffs that were covered in fur

Not fur

But you know what I mean

Flowers

It was just these cliffs

But they were covered in scrubby flowers

And sometimes the flowers would just fall away

And there would be red dust

Like sand

But finer and heavier

FRANCIS. Uh-huh

SANDRA. These gorgeous bald patches

Of just

Dust

FRANCIS. That sounds...magical

SANDRA. It was like I was on an alien planet

I felt like I was a, you know

Alien

That somehow I had crash-landed –

My spaceship!

Had crash-landed

And I was waking up

With wobbly legs

And just

Looking at this *planet*

Where the ground was covered *in purple*

FRANCIS. Oh my god

SANDRA. Purple with red dust

And the mist!

Oh my god

It was something from like

A computer game

This mist...

> *She puts her hands up, trying to remember the mist.*

SANDRA. It just sat in the air

...

And it was raining

Oh my god it was *pouring*

And everyone was stopping their cars to say to me: Honey! What are you doing out in *the rain*?

Cuz someone had died hiking that way I think not too long before

I can't remember who it was

I think like this dude

Had actually died

Because the mist came on so thick

And he was, you know, arrogant

And he just got lost

So all these people

All these *old men*

SANDRA. Were stopping their cars as I was trekking up
the side of the road

My feet knee-high in heather

Saying, "You need a lift?"

And I say, "No"

And I'm just drenched

Wearing a plastic sack

And I am just so happy

And a little scared

And just laughing

Like every time these old men stop

I just laugh

Because they are so worried about me getting lost

And I'm like: I've never been better

I've been living in a fog *for eighteen years*

And this is the best day of my life!

In this rain

I mean, I'm telling you, I was *soaked*, I was *shivering*

And I find these sheep

And I just start laughing with these sheep

And I'm yelling: Heathcliff! Heathcliff!

Because in high school I was *obsessed* with
Wuthering Heights

FRANCIS. *Yessss*

SANDRA. I just thought it was the saddest story

Because he loves her

But it's sooo destructive

And I'm just yelling: HEATHCLIFF

HEAAAATHCLIFFFFFF

In the middle of this storm

As loud as I can

With these sheep watching me

And my heart was just –

Oh my god.

My heart was just like <*bursting*>

And I remember thinking to myself:

Wow. You are so happy

You have never been so alone

You know

No phone

No email

No friends

No family

And you are *so happy*

And it was like there were *two people* inside of me

And they liked each other

They liked each other so much

Like I was walking around with this awesome companion

Inside my body

Everywhere I went

FRANCIS. I used to feel the same way about Jesus

SANDRA. And this was back before. This was back before *everything*. Before I knew *anything about anything*. Oh my god. When I think about it now... I still had *so long to go*

FRANCIS. ...

SANDRA. And I'm always trying to get back

To that moment

Because that girl

That person

Would like

Tell people what's up, you know?

That person

Would like

Know what to do

She wouldn't put up with any of this shit you know

She would just walk out the door

Even if it was five in the morning

...
...

And I know it's not my fault

FRANCIS. No

SANDRA. But I just miss that person so, so much

> *KYLE has entered the restaurant. He watches SHAREEN watch the women talking. She notices him watching her.*

> *In the window – outside the restaurant – WITCHY WITCH is watching KYLE.*

KYLE. Hey

SHAREEN. Hey

KYLE. Sorry I'm late

5.2

KYLE and SHAREEN are having lunch. This is good! They're friends!

WITCHY WITCH is still watching them suspiciously in the window.

SHAREEN. I haven't gone out for pizza in –

...

...

I don't know

I don't know if I really go out for pizza

I think I just eat the dollar slice on-the-go

I don't really sit down. And eat pizza

Anymore

KYLE. Oh my god I go out for pizza all the time

Stuffing their faces.

SHAREEN. Like we used to go out

With my family

And have pizza

It was like. A thing

KYLE. What kind did you get?

SHAREEN. Canadian Bacon, mushrooms, and black olives

KYLE. Huh

SHAREEN. I don't know how we came up with that

But that was the kind we always got

...

...

I feel like it was a big discussion, you know

To arrive at that particular type of pizza

And then once we voted on it

We never changed it again

KYLE. Pepperoni

SHAREEN. Yeah?

KYLE. My family was very simple

Just half cheese. And half pepperoni

SHAREEN. I kind of wish I'd come from a family like that.
Agh. I need to call my mom...

KYLE. Look at us! Out in public! Like normal people

SHAREEN. We're doing so good!

KYLE. Do you want more

SHAREEN. Um

...

...

Yes

Yesss!

KYLE. Let's just finish this whole thing

SHAREEN. Yes!

KYLE. I thought maybe we'd take some home

SHAREEN. No!

KYLE. But let's just eat it

SHAREEN. LET'S GO CRAZY AND EAT IT ALL

They each take another slice.

KYLE. This girl I'm sort of seeing right now

  She always wants to go out for pizza and Oreos

  Like she makes me go to the deli

  To buy her a pack of Oreos

  So that she can eat them with her pizza

  She likes the meat kind

  You know

  Meat lover's pizza

  And Oreos

  At the same time

  It's so funny

SHAREEN. Hey Kyle?

KYLE. Yeah?

SHAREEN. Let's not talk about sex

KYLE. Oh sorry

SHAREEN. No I don't mind

  I just don't really want to talk about it right now

KYLE. Yeah, sorry

  I wasn't thinking

SHAREEN. ...

KYLE. ...

SHAREEN. ...

KYLE. I thought you would think it was funny

He sucks the last drop out of his Diet Coke.
And then tries to scoop up the little chips of
ice with his straw and eat them.

KYLE. *(Ice in his mouth.)* The cold of the ice is piercing
my bone

  SHAREEN looks at her phone. It's ringing.

SHAREEN. Ah, fuck. I need to take this.

  She picks up. KYLE waves her on.

SHAREEN. Hello? ....

 ....

Oh, hi. How are you?

 ....

I'm good, I'm good

 .... *(To KYLE, mouthing the words, rolling her eyes.)* <Sorry>

KYLE. <It's fine>

  KYLE plays with his ice.

  SHAREEN talks on the phone. Her conversation
  makes them both miserable.

SHAREEN. Oh no that's such great news! ....Oh,
no. Thank you for calling me...............I'm so happy.
That's really great

 ....
 ....
 ...

Ohhh, I'm so happy. Thank you. Thank you so much

 ....

---

* A license to produce *Shhhh* does not include a license to publicly display
any branded logos or trademarked images. Licensees must acquire rights
for any logos and/or images or create their own.

....

That's so exciting! ......

......

Tell them how happy I am and how much I –

...

......

....

Yeah. Just tell them I'm really excited...............

.... *(To KYLE.) <Sorry!>*

....

That's so great

...

......

Okay...Okay, I will......

......

....

......

Oh, I'm so happy

...

...

Okay

....

Talk to you later

...

Bye.

KYLE. Good news?

　　　SHAREEN shrugs.

SHAREEN. Stupid television stuff

KYLE. ...

SHAREEN. They just want me for this thing. It's dumb

They play with their straws.

SHAREEN. How's MSNBC going?

KYLE. It's going fine...

SHAREEN. You still doing improv?

KYLE. Not really

SHAREEN. ...

KYLE. ...

SHAREEN. ...

Do you ever do that? Look at the phone? Right when it's ringing.

KYLE. Sometimes

SHAREEN. I'm always doing that. I think I might be magic

KYLE. Or you're just always looking at your phone

SHAREEN. *(Chewing her straw; afraid to look at him.)* Yeah maybe

...
...

Or magic

KYLE. Yeah, I don't know

...
...
...
...
...

SHAREEN. Hey Kyle. Can I ask you a favor?

KYLE. Maybe

SHAREEN. It's a pretty big favor... We'd have to go to like, um... A private place

He stops playing with his straw.

KYLE. What kind of favor?

SHAREEN. ....I know we're not talking about *sex* but...

KYLE. I don't have a problem talking about sex. You're the one who *apparently* has a problem talking about sex...

SHAREEN. I know

But, um

I think maybe I don't have a problem talking about sex right *now*.

Just for a second...

KYLE. ...

SHAREEN. And there's something that I've, um

Been thinking about and –

I know that we're like doing great

Like this is great

Like this is so much better

Than what we were doing before, which –

(I don't want to talk about that, actually.)

But since that's all *over*

And we're doing so great

There's actually something that *I kinda* **want**...

Like pretty badly

And I figured you might give it to me

Because you're crazy

SHAREEN.

...

...

...

And because you owe me

...

...

Like big time owe me

...

...

...

And because you deserve it

...

...

KYLE is intrigued.

KYLE. What is it?

SHAREEN whispers in KYLE's ear.

KYLE. Haha I don't know

...

...

...

...   *(he looks at her – totally aroused and*
                             totally terrified)

...

...

That's not really my type of thing...

WITCHY WITCH still staring through the
window as they exit.

5.3

KYLE and SHAREEN stand facing each other in a private place. They are both terrified and mortified.

SHAREEN. Oh wow. This is weird

KYLE. I know

SHAREEN shuts her eyes and blushes.

SHAREEN. I'm really not used to being on this end of the equation. I feel too embarrassed

KYLE. *You* feel embarrassed

SHAREEN. Maybe this was a bad idea

They stand there for a long time, absolutely electric and feeling awful.

KYLE puts his hands on her shoulders and sort of slowly trails them down her body until he's kneeling on the floor between her legs. She slowly sits in a chair.

SHAREEN. Oh man. We're doing this

He slowly crawls up her leg and over her leg until he's hooked over her knee.

SHAREEN. Oh man. I'm not sure I can do this

She pulls down his pants.

SHAREEN. Oh man

She pulls down his underwear.

SHAREEN. Oh man. I can't believe I'm doing this

KYLE. Shareen. Stop talking

She starts to spank him viciously.

SHAREEN. Oh man

Oh man

OH MAN

OH! MAN!

She spanks him for a long time.

6.

KYLE stumbles out into the streets – tear-streaked and trembling. He reaches for his mobile device. He reaches for his headphones. He puts the earbuds in his ears. his hands are shaking.

He listens to her soothing voice...a barely audible whisper; lips, teeth smacking.

WITCHY WITCH.

Hello there

...

...

<the voice is smiling>

I'm going to give you a massage right now

...

...

So just

Be sure

to

relaxxxxx

...

...

Don't worry

...

...

Don't worry about

...

a single thing

...

...

...

Don't let anything bother you right now

This is your time

To *relaxxxxxx*

...

You earned it

...

...

...

I'm going to give you a head massage

...

I'm going to start from the base of your scalp

...

And work my way through

...

Giving you the best possible

Head Massage

Possible

<a long time listening to the sound of her fingers in someone's hair; fingers brushing against the scalp>

It feels good, huh?

...

...

...

...

I'm glad

<the sound of the scalp massage continues>

I love when people rub their hands through my scalp

...

...

...

Mmmmmm

It feels really good

I agree

...

...

...

And now I'm going to give you a little itch

On your scalp

Just a little itch...

<the sound of her fingernails itching a scalp>

I love it when people make me feel good

...

...

Do you like to make people feel good?

...

...

Or are you selfish?

...

...

...

...

...

Sometimes I find

That the people who *think* they're most generous

Are really the most selfish

...

They're just better at manipulating people than everybody else to get what they want without having to ask for it

<the sound of fingernails itching a scalp continues>

Okay, now I'm just going to rub your forehead

Give you a nice little forehead massage

...

...

Massage your templessssss

...

Like you deserve it

<the sound of someone rubbing someone's forehead; their temples>

I want you to breathe in and out

...

...

...

Good, that's so good...

...

...

Doesn't it feel good just to breathe

...

Doesn't it feel good just to let go?

...

...

And exist?

...

For a change?

<the sound of breath; the sound of someone rubbing someone's forehead>

...

...

...

...

Now I'm going to interrupt our usual programming

...

For a second

...

...

I want you to go deep inside yourself

...

...

And I'm going to ask you a question

...

...

...

Is that okay, if I ask you a question?

...

It's kind of a personal question...

...

...

...

...

...

Do you mind?

...

...

...

...

...

...

...

...

...

...

...

...

...

...

...

...

...

...

...

...

...

...

...

...

...

...

...

...

...

...

...

...

...

...

Are you a rapist?

...

Are you really *not* a rapist?

...

Are you sure?

...

...

...

...

...

...

...

...

I don't know...

You might be a rapist...

...

...

...

...

Have you ever stuck your dick inside somebody without asking?

...

Just the tip?

...

Just the tip, tip, tip?

...

...

...

...

...

I want you to think about my question

...

...

...

...

This is a bag of lavender seeds

<the sound of a bag of lavender seeds>

I'm going to rub them very slowly all over your forehead

...

All over your head

<the sound of a bag of lavender seeds being rubbed all over somebody's head>

Mmmmm

...

Feels nice

...

Smells nice

...

I love it when things that feel nice, smell nice

...

Are you thinking about my question?

...

...

...

...

...

...

...

<the sound of a bag of lavender seeds being rubbed all over somebody's head>

One thing I forgot to tell you

...

...

...

I'm a witch

And I'm going to come for you in the night

When you least expect it

And cut off your dick

...

...

...

...

Just the tip

...

Just the tip, tip, tip

...

...

...

<the sound of a bag of lavender seeds being rubbed all over somebody's head>

Live in fear

As you have made me live in fear

...

...

...

...

...

KYLE alone, trembling, in the afternoon light.

7.

WITCHY WITCH enters, bedecked in ceremonial robes – everything but the hat. It's sunset. She prepares the space – drawing a circle on the ground with chalk. Setting out candles. This can take some time.

The sun gets a little lower in the sky.

SHAREEN enters, out of breath.

SHAREEN. I'm so sorry I'm so late

WITCHY WITCH. It's okay

SHAREEN. Have you started?

WITCHY WITCH. Just setting up the meditation ritual

SHAREEN. Where is everyone?

WITCHY WITCH shrugs.

WITCHY WITCH. I don't know if anybody's coming

I advertised it on Facebook

But no one clicked "yes"

SHAREEN. Oh, Sally. I'm sorry

WITCHY WITCH. I just thought it would be a nice thing

SHAREEN. It *is* a nice thing

You just haven't found your audience yet

WITCHY WITCH starts to light the candles.

SHAREEN. Do you need help?

WITCHY WITCH. Nah, I'm good

SHAREEN watches her.

WITCHY WITCH . I called you earlier

SHAREEN. Oh, shit. I'm sorry

WITCHY WITCH. ...

SHAREEN. I was with a friend

   ...

   ...

   Everything okay?

WITCHY WITCH. Just checking in

SHAREEN. ...

WITCHY WITCH. Everything okay with you?

SHAREEN. Yeah, I'm good

   ...

   ...

   ...

   Just a...weird afternoon

WITCHY WITCH. ...

SHAREEN. ...

WITCHY WITCH. ...

SHAREEN. How was your *date*?

WITCHY WITCH. I don't think they liked me

SHAREEN. I'm sure they liked you. What did they say?

WITCHY WITCH. They were shy

   ...

   ...

   ...

   They said they had some more free time in September

SHAREEN. That's good

      *SHAREEN has made her way over to a giant
      urn.*

SHAREEN. What are these?

WITCHY WITCH. Lavender seeds. We were going to scatter them

SHAREEN. We still can

WITCHY WITCH. Shareen, I have to tell you something

SHAREEN. ...

WITCHY WITCH. I applied to be transferred to the forensics department. Of the post office. In Salt Lake City

SHAREEN. Salt Lake City!

WITCHY WITCH. Job opportunities are booming out there. Because of the Mormons, I guess

SHAREEN. I bet that's true

WITCHY WITCH. I asked the HR woman about dating because I was wondering if it'd be a friendly kind of atmosphere and she said there's lots of ex-Mormons to choose from

They put it in their profiles: Ex-LDS

Not that I wouldn't date a Mormon

Or I guess, it's true, I wouldn't date a Mormon

Or at least a good Mormon

I might date a bad one

SHAREEN. So you're going to do it???

WITCHY WITCH. Well, they haven't called me yet...

SHAREEN. That's so exciting!

...
...
...
...

Ah! I'm going to be in the city all alone. My closest family will be two thousand miles away.

WITCHY WITCH. You could always come with me, you know

SHAREEN.

...

...

...

WITCHY WITCH. We could get a little cabin. Live like two spinsters deep in the woods...

SHAREEN.

...

...

...

I don't want you to go

WITCHY WITCH. ...

SHAREEN. ...

WITCHY WITCH. ...

SHAREEN. ...

WITCHY WITCH. Shareen?

SHAREEN. Yes?

WITCHY WITCH. I have to ask you a favor

> *She pulls out a worn, yellowed letter from her robes.*

WITCHY WITCH. Would you help me get rid of this letter?

Louis Gonzalo

I feel so bad. I can't do it

SHAREEN. Who is Louis Gonzalo

WITCHY WITCH. I don't know

I took that letter from him and he never got it

SHAREEN. You stole it!

WITCHY WITCH. I didn't steal it

I just didn't give it back. It's been twenty years

SHAREEN. Sally!

WITCHY WITCH. I know

I'm so ashamed. It's been haunting me

SHAREEN. Well, give it back now

WITCHY WITCH. How am I supposed to find him?

SHAREEN. There's an address

WITCHY WITCH. It's from twenty years ago

SHAREEN. It's a place to start

WITCHY WITCH. He'll know that I kept it

SHAREEN. You don't have to say that

WITCHY WITCH. No, I should. I should say that. I should be honest

> *SHAREEN snatches the letter.*

> *She dips it in the flame of a candle.*

WITCHY WITCH. Wait –

SHAREEN. What?

WITCHY WITCH. No!

SHAREEN. You said to get rid of it –

WITCHY WITCH. I changed my mind! I think we should give it to him!

> *The letter burns up.*

SHAREEN. It doesn't matter

...

It's old

...
...
...
...

SHAREEN. Besides, I think sometimes it's okay to make bad things disappear

> *The letter burns to ash. The sisters stand in their candle circle, all alone.*

WITCHY WITCH. Nobody's coming...

SHAREEN. People always come late

...

WITCHY WITCH. ...

SHAREEN. ...

WITCHY WITCH. Well, thank you for being here. At least

SHAREEN. Of course

WITCHY WITCH. You always come

SHAREEN. Of course, I do!

WITCHY WITCH. I know. But it means a lot

> *They stand there – an arm around each hip.*

WITCHY WITCH. Should we get started?

SHAREEN. We can wait!

WITCHY WITCH. No, I want to get started

> *She starts to set up shop in the middle of the circle – various mysterious bottles and things. A small cauldron.*

WITCHY WITCH. I was going to do a little thing for the full moon but now I'm just gonna do a little something for you and me. Sit down

They sit. WITCHY WITCH reaches into her bag.

WITCHY WITCH. Take some of this

She hands SHAREEN whiskey.

WITCHY WITCH. Take it in your mouth

SHAREEN takes it in her mouth.

WITCHY WITCH. Spit it in this urn

SHAREEN spits.

WITCHY WITCH. Do it again

SHAREEN takes more whiskey and spits.

WITCHY WITCH. And again.

SHAREEN takes more whiskey and spits.

WITCHY WITCH. Okay, me too

WITCHY WITCH spits.

WITCHY WITCH. Chew this with your mouth

She hands SHAREEN a fistful of nettle leaf.

SHAREEN. What is it?

WITCHY WITCH. Nettle leaf

SHAREEN chews.

WITCHY WITCH. And spit

SHAREEN spits.

Witchy Witch hands her a small carton.

WITCHY WITCH. Take this goat's milk

SHAREEN takes the goat's milk into her mouth.

WITCHY WITCH. Spit

SHAREEN does. The milk dribbles down her chin.

WITCHY WITCH takes the milk into her mouth, too. It dribbles down her chin, too.

WITCHY WITCH. Now there's supposed to be blood

SHAREEN. Wait, actually

...

One second

...

...

...

SHAREEN reaches up inside her skirt and digs around discreetly for her DivaCup.*

WITCHY WITCH looks over her shoulder to see if anybody's watching.

WITCHY WITCH. Hurry up

SHAREEN pulls out her DivaCup. There's a little blood in it.

She pours it in the cauldron.

WITCHY WITCH. Now we stir, or rather, froth it

SHAREEN. *Lol*

WITCHY WITCH froths the cauldron.

---

* A license to produce *Shhhh* does not include a license to publicly display any branded logos or trademarked images. Licensees must acquire rights for any logos and/or images or create their own.

SHAREEN. What's it for

WITCHY WITCH. I'm going to tell you

>   *WITCHY WITCH stops frothing.*

WITCHY WITCH. *(Pointed.)* Alcohol for letting go of bad choices. Bad people in your life

SHAREEN. Haha okay

WITCHY WITCH. Nettle leaf so we can sit with things that are uncomfortable

SHAREEN. All right

WITCHY WITCH. And not expect them to pass

SHAREEN. Good...

WITCHY WITCH. Goat's milk for the erotic as it pertains to the goddess

SHAREEN. Makes sense

WITCHY WITCH. Blood for vengeance against anyone who harms us

>   *SHAREEN reaches across and plucks one of WITCHY WITCH's hairs.*

SHAREEN. And this is for protection for when we're far apart

WITCHY WITCH. *Oh!*

>   *SHAREEN drinks the potion.*

>   *WITCHY WITCH drinks the potion.*

WITCHY WITCH. Now we scatter the lavender seeds.

>   *SHAREEN reaches into the bag of lavender seeds and throws them above their heads.*

>   *She throws some more.*

*WITCHY WITCH cranks the boombox. Cheesy chanting music comes booming out.**

They throw lavender seeds all over the stage – sweeping arcs of confetti. Angry pellets raining down.

It becomes a sort of primal dance – the witchy chanting music still going. The lavender seeds flying everywhere. It morphs into something strange and angry. An exorcism of sorts.

A sheep appears.

SHAREEN carries the sheep like a baby.

The moon comes out.

SHAREEN with the sheep, under the moon...

SHAREEN.

I went to the doctor the other week. I've been so sick. For about a year now. First it was strep. Then it was mono. Then I got an amoebic infection because the mono made me weak. My back was breaking out, I had cystic pimples all along my jaw. I started getting nosebleeds. My palms would have these itching attacks in the middle of the night, and I would get out of my bed and drag them across the sharp points of the counters, desperate to get some relief. I started thinking about suicide all the time. In a casual way. Maybe six to nine times a day. Just thinking: Gosh. Wouldn't it be nice, if this were over. I'd take long walks along the highway, thinking about throwing myself into traffic. My dermatologist was the first one who

---

*A license to produce *Shhhh* does not include a performance license for any third-party or copyrighted music. Licensees should create an original composition or use music in the public domain. For further information, please see the Music and Third-Party Materials Use Note on page iii.

said it to me, she said: Shareen, I think all of this – the mono and the nosebleeds and the cystic pimples and the viral infection I got that made my asshole erupt into tiny pin-sized warts – this all might be *emotional*. Emotional problems. Kyle was very compassionate. He was falling in love with me at the time. All I wanted, in retrospect, was for him to think I was sexy. I realized I would do anything he asked of me. I would cut my body open and let him stick his dick inside of the wound. And I didn't even like him that much. I am a machine for other people's desires. And I don't quite know how that happened or how to make it stop.

8.

A knock at the door. It's late. WITCHY WITCH opens the door. It's PENNY.

PENNY. Hi

WITCHY WITCH. Hello...

PENNY. Can I come in?

WITCHY WITCH lets them in. PENNY's wearing some kind of fabulous dress – space-alien disco.

PENNY. I was wondering, if you would do the electricity thing to me. Like you told me about

WITCHY WITCH. If you want me to...?

PENNY. Yes please

WITCHY WITCH hesitates...

WITCHY WITCH. Do you want some tea? Or maybe some water?

PENNY. No, I'm okay

WITCHY WITCH. I have little cookies?

PENNY. Haha no thanks

> *WITCHY WITCH goes to get the contraption.*
> *It's buried in an old cardboard box – ancient*
> *and soft. She looks back over her shoulder...*

WITCHY WITCH. You look nice

PENNY. *(Shy, laughing.)* I was at a party

WITCHY WITCH. Associated Foods???

> *WITCHY WITCH approaches PENNY with*
> *the contraption.*
>
> *She unpacks it, carefully, peanuts going*
> *everywhere, uncoiling a bright-orange*
> *extension cord, and then handing PENNY*
> *some kind of luminescent, gummy wand.*

WITCHY WITCH. *(To PENNY.)* Hold onto this

> *PENNY stares at the wand, curious, as*
> *WITCHY WITCH plugs it in and then tucks*
> *the metal pedal into the waistband of her*
> *pants, so that her fingertips become electric...*

WITCHY WITCH. I'm going to start with it really gentle,
don't be nervous

> *PENNY nods.*
>
> *WITCHY WITCH touches PENNY all over*
> *– up-and-down their arms, their neck, their*
> *tongue, inside their mouth...*
>
> *WITCHY WITCH adjusts the dial...*

WITCHY WITCH. Does that feel alright?

> *PENNY nods.*

PENNY. I think I smell something burning...

WITCHY WITCH. That's just your baby hairs

PENNY. *(Nervous.)* Don't actually hurt me?

WITCHY WITCH. I won't, hunny, I won't

> *It's dark, and we can see the little blue worms leaping between WITCHY WITCH's fingers and PENNY's skin.*

PENNY. You can turn it up

WITCHY WITCH. Are you sure?

> *PENNY nods.*

WITCHY WITCH. Tell me when

> *PENNY braces themselves – it starts to hurt a little.*

PENNY. That's good

> *PENNY takes their top down, and WITCHY WITCH gently touches PENNY on their nipples.*

...

......

....

PENNY. I think I like it

WITCHY WITCH. You think you do?

PENNY. Yeah

> *PENNY shudders.*

PENNY. I think I like the way it feels

> *This continues...*

> *SHAREEN alone in her house. She calls her mom.*

SHAREEN. Hi Mom

...

...

...

How are you doing?

...

...

I'm fine. I was just calling to chat. I'm sorry I haven't called you sooner. I've been meaning to...

...

...

> *Blood is dripping down SHAREEN's face. She has a bloody nose. She notices it dripping.*

SHAREEN. Hold on one second, my nose is bleeding...

...

...

No it just does this sometimes

> *SHAREEN holds a wad of tissue to her nose.*

SHAREEN. Okay, I'm back with you. How are *you* doing?

> *She laughs.*

SHAREEN. I don't know

...

...

...

I don't want to talk about me, I want to talk about *you.*

I'm fine. It's boring

...

...

> *She laughs.*

SHAREEN. I don't know

...
...
...

Tell me about the deer

...
...

Tell me about the baby

...
...

Tell me about the cousins

...
...

Tell me about what's going on in church

...
...

Tell me about what's going on in the school district

...
...

Tell me about what's going on with your diabetes

...
...

Tell me about what's going on in your garden

...
...

Tell me about what you do when you're all alone

...
...
...

And SHAREEN'S MOM tells her about the deer and the baby and the cousins and the school district. She tells her about her diabetes and her garden. And how the hawks ate the baby ducks and the Japanese maple bush died. And how Anthony took her to the grocery store to help her lift her grocery bags.

And she says: Sometimes I think about you and your sister. Living in the city. And I think about all the people you see. And all the things you do. And I think about you and your television work. And your sister in the vestibule of other people's houses. And all the parties. And all the late nights. And all the cups of coffee. And smells of garbage. And smells of bakeries. And smells of morning. And I think:

You girls are leading such extraordinary lives.

And the stage gets darker and darker until all we can see is the blue worms leaping between finger and skin.

End